AUDREY WOOD **THE NAPPING**

Illustrated by **DON WOOD HOUSE**

HARCOURT, INC.

Orlando   Austin   New York   San Diego   Toronto

www.HarcourtBooks.com

The Library of Congress has cataloged an earlier edition as follows:
Wood, Audrey.
The napping house.
Summary: In this cumulative tale, a wakeful flea atop a number of
sleeping creatures causes a commotion, with just one bite.
[1. Sleep—Fiction.   2. Fleas—Fiction.]   I. Wood, Don, 1945– ill.
II. Title.
PZ7.W846Na   1984
[E]   83-13035
ISBN 0-15-256708-9 hc
ISBN 0-15-205080-9 book and CD

First Harcourt book-and-musical-CD edition 2004
H G F E D C B A

The original paintings were done in oil on pressed board.
The text is Clearface Roman, set by Thomson Type,
    San Diego, California.
The display type is Clearface Bold, set by Thompson Type,
    San Diego, California.
Color separations by Heinz Weber, Inc., Los Angeles, California
Printed and bound by Tien Wah Press, Singapore
This book was printed on totally chlorine-free Stora Enso Matte paper.
Production supervision by Sandra Grebenar and Ginger Boyer
Designed by Dalia Hartman

Printed in Singapore

For Maegerine Thompson Brewer

There is a house,
a napping house,
where everyone is sleeping.

And in that house
there is a bed,
a cozy bed
in a napping house,
where everyone is sleeping.

And on that bed
there is a granny,
a snoring granny
on a cozy bed
in a napping house,
where everyone is sleeping.

And on that granny
there is a child,
a dreaming child
on a snoring granny
on a cozy bed
in a napping house,
where everyone is sleeping.

And on that child
there is a dog,
a dozing dog
on a dreaming child
on a snoring granny
on a cozy bed
in a napping house,
where everyone is sleeping.

And on that dog
there is a cat,
a snoozing cat
on a dozing dog
on a dreaming child
on a snoring granny
on a cozy bed
in a napping house,
where everyone is sleeping.

And on that cat
there is a mouse,
a slumbering mouse
on a snoozing cat
on a dozing dog
on a dreaming child
on a snoring granny
on a cozy bed
in a napping house,
where everyone is sleeping.

And on that mouse
there is a flea. . . .

Can it be?
A wakeful flea
on a slumbering mouse
on a snoozing cat
on a dozing dog
on a dreaming child
on a snoring granny
on a cozy bed
in a napping house,
where everyone is sleeping.

A wakeful flea
who bites the mouse,

who scares the cat,

who claws the dog,

who thumps the child,

who bumps the granny,

who breaks the bed,

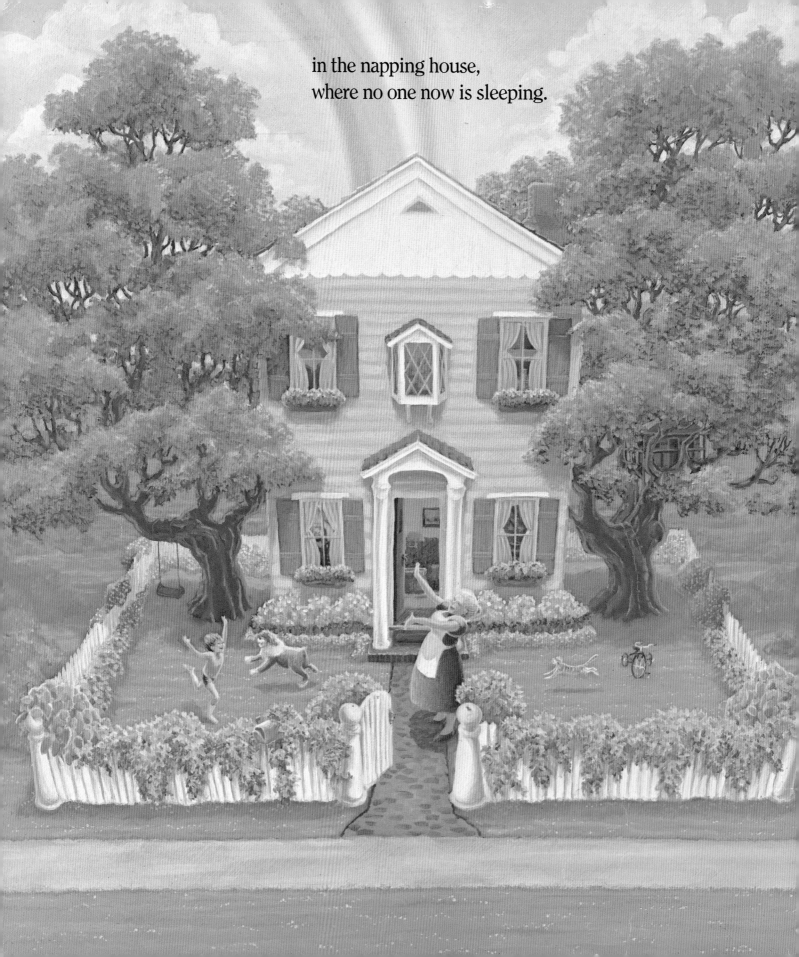

in the napping house,
where no one now is sleeping.